Odd one out

Jenny Tyler and Robyn Gee
Designed and illustrated by Graham Round

With consultant advice from Gillian Hartley and John Newson
of the Child Development Research Unit at Nottingham University.

About this book

This book is for an adult and child to use together.
Its aim is to give children practice in noticing
similarities and differences. Looking at groups of
objects and matching like with like helps children
develop basic reasoning skills which contribute to
much that they will need to learn later,
including maths and reading.

Notes for parents

It is important to use this book when both you and your child are in the right mood to enjoy it and not to try to do too much at one time. Short, frequent sessions will allow the child's concentration to build up gradually. Leave any activities your child seems unready or unwilling to tackle and come back to them later.

Asking questions

The questions given throughout the book are intended as starting points for discussion. You can develop the ideas further by asking questions of your own and encouraging your child to tell you why something is the odd one out.

Discussion about which things are the same and which are different encourages the child to understand the basis of logical classification which underlines all later thinking with both words and numbers.

Why odd one out?

Learning about similarities and differences between groups of objects is essential to any child's early conceptual development. By finding out which objects do *not* belong in a given category, children are enlarging their understanding of how words are often used to refer to whole classes of objects rather than as labels for particular things.

The first part of the book concentrates on similarities and differences based on size, shape, colour and orientation. Differences depending on more difficult concepts are introduced later in the book. These require the child to be able to group objects according to criteria based on a more advanced understanding of language.

Pens and pencils

There are plenty of colouring opportunities in this book and your child will need a set of crayons or felt pens for these. Colouring is not only a very satisfying activity but is also a valuable way of helping develop good pencil control.

So before you start, check your child is holding the pen or pencil correctly. It is easy to develop bad writing habits with the wrong grip.

Pens and pencils should be held lightly between the thumb and first two fingers, about 2cm from the point.

Some activities involve drawing lines to join pairs of objects. With these, it is a good idea to get children to trace in the lines with a finger first before attempting to do them with a pen or pencil.

Ideas for follow-up activities

You could follow up any of the pages in this book with practical activities, such as making collections of objects which include an odd one out – plastic farm animals plus one wild one or vegetables plus one fruit for example.

You could also make a collection of objects such as a fork, cup, pencil and so on and ask your child to search for things to go with them.

There are several games which involve making pairs and groups, such as snap, happy families and pelmanism. You could remove one of the cards from a pack of snap cards and ask your child to sort them into pairs to find the odd card out.

Colour

- One flower is different from the others. Colour its centre.

- Which butterfly is not the same as the others? Draw a circle round it.

- Which snake is the odd one out? Colour it to make it like the others.

- Which dinosaur is the odd one out? Draw a hat on it.

3

Size

- Which teddy is the odd one out? Colour it.

- Which cup is the odd one out? Colour it.

- Which plate is the odd one out? Colour it.

- Which spoon is the odd one out? Colour it.

- Which cake is the odd one out? Colour it.

4

Shape

- Look at all the different things in this picture.
  There is one thing of each type that is a different shape to the others.

- Find all the odd ones out and draw circles round them.

- Finish colouring the picture.

Colour, size and shape

- Which gnome is the odd one out? Colour his hat.

- Which butterfly is the odd one out? Colour it in.

- Which bee and fish are the odd ones out?
  Draw circles round them.

Matching pairs

- Find a pair for each animal and colour their umbrellas to match.

- Can you find an animal which doesn't have a pair? Draw one for it.

Matching shapes

- Cat and mouse are wrapping up presents.

- Draw lines to join the objects to their parcels.

- Colour the labels of each pair to match.

- Which object doesn't have a parcel?
Can you draw a parcel for it?

Drawing strings

- Draw a string from each kite to a rabbit. Does each rabbit have a kite?
- Draw a kite for the rabbit who doesn't have one.

- Draw a string from each boat to a teddy. Is there a boat for each teddy?
- Draw a boat for the teddy who doesn't have one.

Shapes maze

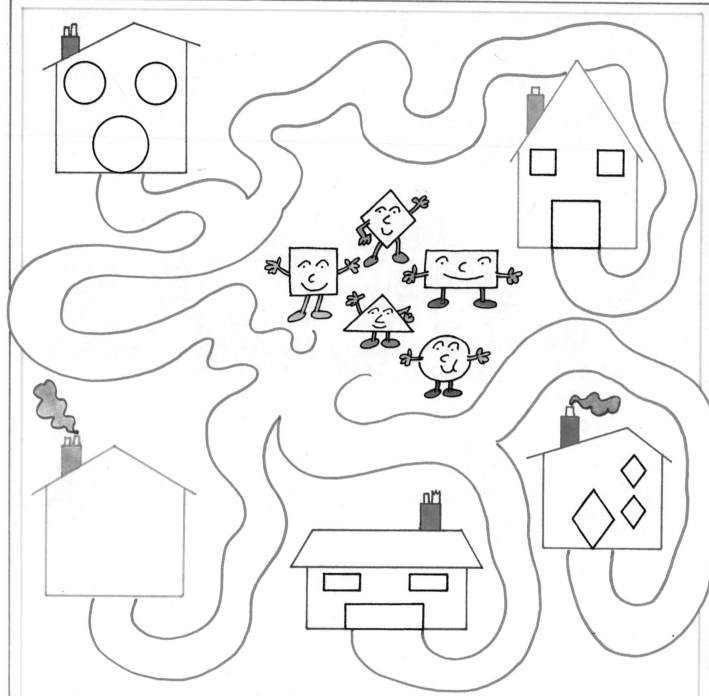

- The shape people live in houses with windows and doors of the same shape as themselves. Where does each shape person live?

- Draw a line to show each shape person which path leads to their home.

- Whose house doesn't have a door or windows? Draw them in.

Things that go together

- Cat has drawn a picture.

- Mouse has found some objects which go with the things in cat's picture.

- One of the objects mouse has found doesn't belong to anything in the picture.
  To find out which it is, draw a line from each object to the thing it belongs to.

- Draw a circle round the odd one out.

Orientation

● Look at each row. Find the one that is different and colour it.

● Look at each row. Find the one that is different and colour it.

What's missing?

- Look at the animals, birds, flowers and insects in this picture. One thing of each type has something missing.

14

● Find each odd one out and draw in what is missing.

Find the pairs

- Cat and mouse are playing a game. Can you help them?

- Draw lines to show which cards belong together.

- What do you think is on the upside-down card? Draw a picture of it here.

Groups of three

- Cat and mouse are sorting things out.
  They have put one thing in each box. Now they want to
  put two more things in each box.

- Draw a coloured circle round each object to match
  the box it belongs in.

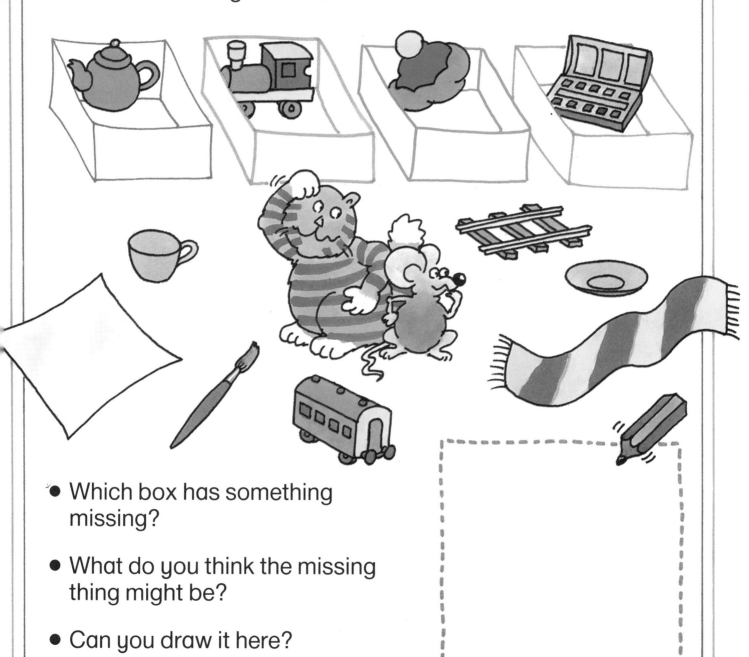

- Which box has something missing?

- What do you think the missing thing might be?

- Can you draw it here?

Odd one out

- In each row above there is an odd one out.
  Can you find it and colour it?

18

● In each row above there is an odd one out.
Can you find it and colour it?

What's out of place?

- Look at the house. There are two things in each room that don't belong.

20

● Can you find all the things that are out of place?
Draw a circle round each one.

Where things come from

- Draw a string from each label to the thing it comes from.

- Which label is the odd one out?

- Draw a picture of the thing it comes from.

Matching sets

- Draw lines to join the sets of the same number.

- Which set is the odd one out? How many things are in it?

- Draw that many snakes in the empty space above.

Count the spots

- Count the spots on each dog.

- Draw lines to join each number to the dog with that number of spots.

- Which number doesn't have a matching dog?

- Draw that number of spots on the blank dog.

- Draw over the numbers.